The Magic School Bus®

GOING BATTY

A BOOK ABOUT BATS

SCHOLASTIC INC.
New York   Toronto   London   Auckland   Sydney
Mexico City   New Delhi   Hong Kong   Buenos Aires

From an episode of the animated TV series
produced by Scholastic Entertainment Inc.
Based on *The Magic School Bus* books
written by Joanna Cole and illustrated by Bruce Degen.

TV tie-in adaptation by Nancy E. Krulik and illustrated by Bob Ostrom.
TV script written by Ronnie Krauss, Brian Meehl, and George Arthur Bloom.

ISBN-10: 0-590-73872-0
ISBN-13: 978-0-590-73872-9

35 34 33 32 31 30 29 28 27   08 09 10 11 12/0

Printed in the U.S.A.

I wonder where Ms. Frizzle will be flying off to tonight.

You never know. I always thought Ms. Frizzle was a little batty.

Our teacher, Ms. Frizzle, loves field trips! In fact, she loves them so much, she even took our parents on one! It all started on Parents Night....

We were all busy putting up our nocturnal animals display in the classroom. Everywhere you looked, there were animals that come out at night — owls, possums, raccoons, and moths. The place looked great. The only thing missing was Ms. Frizzle, and our parents would be there any minute.

Suddenly the classroom door swung open and a stranger rushed in!

Poor Arnold — he thought the visitor was a real vampire! But it was only Ralphie in disguise. Ralphie pulled off his mask and laughed.

"Knock it off, Ralphie," Keesha scolded him. "There are no such things as vampires."

Ralphie shook his head. "That's what you think," he argued. "Bats are just vampires in disguise." And to prove it, Ralphie read to us from his vampire comic book.

"The vampire looked around the room of half humans–half bats and said, 'Attention, my beloved children, at last the moment I've been waiting for is here.'"

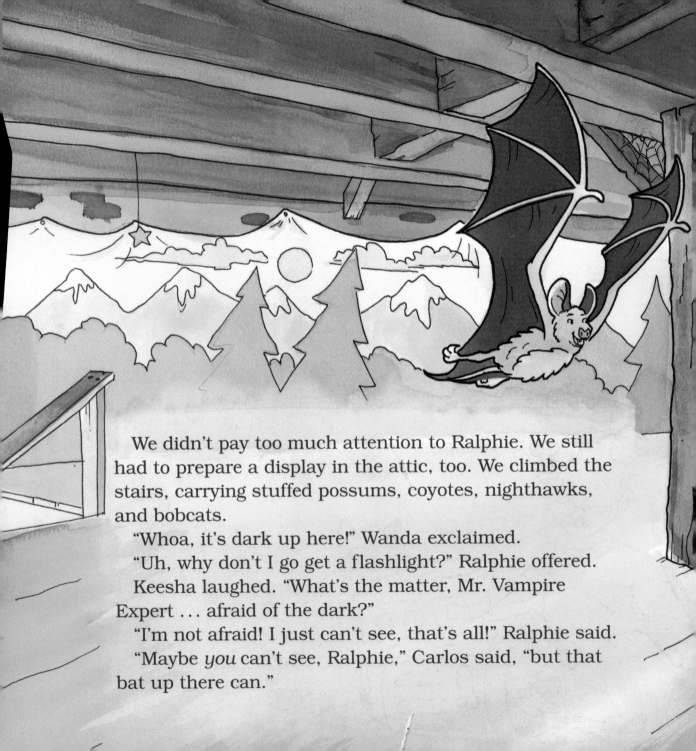

We didn't pay too much attention to Ralphie. We still had to prepare a display in the attic, too. We climbed the stairs, carrying stuffed possums, coyotes, nighthawks, and bobcats.

"Whoa, it's dark up here!" Wanda exclaimed.

"Uh, why don't I go get a flashlight?" Ralphie offered.

Keesha laughed. "What's the matter, Mr. Vampire Expert . . . afraid of the dark?"

"I'm not afraid! I just can't see, that's all!" Ralphie said.

"Maybe *you* can't see, Ralphie," Carlos said, "but that bat up there can."

A small brown bat hung upside down from one of the attic beams. The little guy was fast asleep.

"Wow!" Dorothy Ann said excitedly. "A real creature of the night!"

Whoosh! The bat awoke and flew right over our heads!

Just then, we heard a creaking noise coming from the wooden beams above. There was a blast of wind. Someone — or something — swung down from above. It was a large creature — half human and half bat!

"Good evening, class!" the creature said in a scary Transylvanian accent.

We all breathed a big sigh of relief. It was just Ms. Frizzle, dressed like a bat lady!

"I see you've found my creature of the night," Ms. Frizzle said, pointing at the bat. "Come. Don't be afraid. Let me show you the secrets of being nocturnal. When you are a creature of the night, you wear the color of night so you won't be seen by your enemies. You stay hidden until the sun has set, and you feed only during the night."

Beep! Beep! Outside, we could hear the Magic School Bus signaling Ms. Frizzle. Our parents had arrived. We were all excited that Ms. Frizzle would finally meet our parents. Except Ralphie, that is. Ralphie was convinced Ms. Frizzle was a vampire.

Ralphie, stop being such a pain in the neck.

You think *I'm* a pain in the neck? Just wait!

"Your attention, please!" Ms. Frizzle called. "I thought for the parents-only portion of the evening we might go someplace a little more breathtaking."

We all stared at her. A field trip for our parents?

Ms. Frizzle turned and headed toward the Magic School Bus. "Come along, I won't bite. And don't you worry about the children ... they'll be taken care of."

That was all Ralphie needed to hear. "Yikes! We're next," he gasped.

"I wonder where Ms. Frizzle's taking them?" Tim asked as he watched our parents drive off in the Magic School Bus.

Vroom! Just then Liz pulled up on a very strange-looking motorcycle — complete with sidecars.

"I don't know," Ralphie replied, leaping into a sidecar, "but we have to find out!"

We each buckled ourselves into a sidecar. With Liz in the driver's seat, we followed the Magic School Bus way into the country and across a narrow road that led to an island. The bus stopped in front of an old, crumbling castle.

Follow that bus!

My thoughts exactly!

We watched through the bushes as Ms. Frizzle opened the castle doors. A swarm of bats zoomed out into the dark night.

"Why would Ms. Frizzle bring our parents to a place full of bats?" Wanda asked.

"And mosquitoes," Dorothy Ann added, swatting at a bug.

"Because she's a vampire, that's why!" Ralphie said.

"Ralphie!" Keesha said. "Ms. Frizzle can't be a vampire, because vampires don't exist. I'm sure there is a perfectly logical explanation for all this, and I'm going to find out what it is!" She ran up to the castle doors.

Wanda tried opening the door — but the knob came off in her hand. We certainly weren't getting into the castle that way.

"Admit it, Ralphie," Keesha said, "this vampire thing is a bunch of junk!"

Ralphie peered into a nearby window. "Oh, yeah? Then explain why Ms. Frizzle is making our parents drink blood!"

Keesha moved over next to Ralphie and looked through the window. "Hold it!" she called back to us. "That's not blood. It's tomato juice."

Carlos slapped at his arm "Get away, you bloodsuckers!" he yelled.

"Vampires?" Ralphie asked nervously.

"No, mosquitoes," Carlos answered.

A few bats swooped down from a nearby tree. "More bats!" Ralphie screamed.

To the creatures of the night. Long may we fly together.

We watched in fear as the bats flew closer and closer. One bat circled above Arnold's head. It opened its mouth and … captured a mosquito in midair!

"The bats don't want to eat *us*," Phoebe said. "They want to eat the mosquitoes."

"Which proves they aren't vampires!" Keesha exclaimed, looking straight at Ralphie.

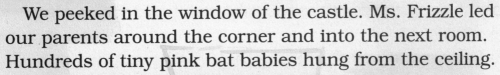

We peeked in the window of the castle. Ms. Frizzle led our parents around the corner and into the next room. Hundreds of tiny pink bat babies hung from the ceiling.

"Aren't those bat babies cute?" Phoebe asked.

Keesha pointed to a mother bat feeding one of her young. "See, Ralphie," she explained, "bats are mammals, not vampires! Their babies drink milk, not blood!"

Ralphie looked through the window. His face turned white.

"Get down!" he whispered. "The Friz is coming."

Ralphie raced across the moonlit courtyard to the Magic School Bus.

"Ralphie, what are you trying to do?" Wanda cried out.

"Get us outta here!" Ralphie called out from the driver's window.

That seemed like a good plan. We followed Ralphie onto the bus.

There was, however, one slight problem with Ralphie's plan ... Ralphie didn't know how to drive. He looked at the dashboard. He spotted a button with a bat on it. Ralphie pushed the button. The bus spun around wildly.

Nice one, Ralphie. You turned the bus into a bat!

The Magic School Bus sprouted black wings. Its
windshield grew eyes, and ears popped up from its fenders.
The Magic School Bus had become the Magic School Bat!

I knew I should have stayed home tonight

It was dark outside. We couldn't see a thing. "What if we crash into something?" Arnold asked.

"Uh-oh! Big trees at twelve o'clock!" Wanda called out.

We didn't need to worry. The bus flew easily between the trees.

"Awesome! How does the bus keep from running into stuff?" Carlos asked.

"It's a bat, that's how," Keesha answered. "It knows how to get around in the dark. I think it has something to do with that pinging sound."

Every time the Magic School Bat opened its mouth, it let out a high-pitched *ping*. Then its ears would wiggle. "I think it's listening to the echo of each ping," Tim said.

"I don't know about you guys, but that pinging is killing my ears!" Arnold moaned. He put on some earmuffs to muffle the sound.

Keesha knew that the pings were really important. "When the sound hits an object and bounces back," she explained, "the bus hears the echo and knows the object is there."

"It uses echoes ... to ... locate," Phoebe thought out loud. "Echolocation! Bats don't need to see with their eyes — they see with their ears!"

"Cool," said Wanda. "Bats use sound to get around!"

"Come on, Ralphie, admit it," Keesha urged. "Bats are cool. And if you were a night animal, you'd want to be one!"

"I would not," Ralphie answered quickly. Then he thought about it. "A bat could fly back to the castle in the dark, find a way inside, and save his parents from Count Frizzula!"

The thought of his mom turning into a vampire made Ralphie so determined that he pushed all the buttons on the dashboard.

Ralphie's finger landed on a button that had a picture of a kid with bat wings on it. Before we knew it, we'd all turned into bats!

"This wasn't exactly what I had in mind," Ralphie admitted.

But the rest of us thought turning into bats was kind of exciting!

YIKES!

Arnold didn't seem to be having any fun. "I wish I could turn off the moon," he said with a shiver. "Its light is giving me the creeps."

Suddenly Carlos screamed out into the darkness. "Owl alert!"

"Owl alert?" Arnold asked.

Just then a great horned owl swooped down from a high tree branch. He tried to use his sharp, strong claws to capture Arnold and Tim!

It was a good thing Arnold and Tim were hanging upside down, because they could move quickly. They flew out of the owl's way, leaving the big bird with nothing to grab but air. Then they headed to a nearby tree, where the rest of us were hanging around.

"That's why we bats avoid light. Our enemies can see us in it," Keesha explained to Arnold and Tim.

What if Ralphie's right and the Friz is a vampire?

I'm trying not to think about that.

"At last the moment I've been waiting for has come!" we heard Ms. Frizzle say. "Prepare yourselves! Who would like to be my first victim?"

"Take me, Ms. Frizzle," one of the grown-ups called out. Keesha could barely believe her supersensitive bat ears. Her grandmother was volunteering to be Ms. Frizzle's victim! Ralphie was right! The Friz *was* a vampire!

Keesha flew into an airshaft that led inside the castle. *"Don't you dare bite my grandmother!"* she cried out.

We couldn't let Keesha battle Count Frizzula alone! We followed her down the shaft and used echolocation to fly safely through the castle.

In the distance, we could hear the grown-ups' voices. "I can't believe I let you do this to me," Keesha's grandmother said.

"My neck will be sore for a week," Ralphie's mother added.

"Maybe we should have stayed home tonight," Arnold's mother groaned.

"Will the kids suffer the same fate we did?" Phoebe's father asked.

The Friz laughed. "Of course. They're mine, too, aren't they?"

"We have to make sure she never does this again!" Ralphie whispered to Keesha.

We zoomed into the next room and discovered...

Ms. Frizzle hadn't turned our parents into bats at all! She had simply shown them how it feels to be a bat, by helping them hang upside down from a chandelier.

Ms. Frizzle, as my Keesha always says, your field trips are simply magical!

Is it just me, or do those bats look like our kids?

She doesn't know the half of it!

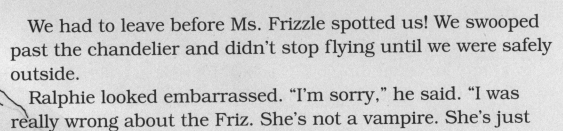

We had to leave before Ms. Frizzle spotted us! We swooped past the chandelier and didn't stop flying until we were safely outside.

Ralphie looked embarrassed. "I'm sorry," he said. "I was really wrong about the Friz. She's not a vampire. She's just a really good teacher who gets wrapped up in her work."

Then Ralphie did something amazing. He admitted he was wrong about bats, too! "Okay, they're not vampires," he said. "They're nocturnal animals that use echolocation to fly at night. They come out at night to feed on insects, not human blood." Ralphie turned to Keesha. "Happy now?" he asked her.

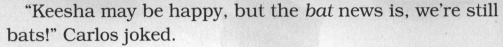

"Keesha may be happy, but the *bat* news is, we're still bats!" Carlos joked.

"*Fangs* for reminding us, Carlos," Phoebe giggled.

Beep! Beep! The Magic School Bus flew by with Liz at the wheel. It stopped just long enough for us to fly on board. Before we knew it, we were transformed from bats back into kids.

"What do you know! It's our kids!" Arnold's father said as he left the castle.

Ralphie's mother looked him squarely in the eye. "I know that guilty look, Ralphie," she said. "What's going on?"

Ms. Frizzle put her arm around Ralphie. "Oh, I'm sure they were just *hanging out*," she answered with a smile.

"Right, Ms. Frizzle," Ralphie agreed. And *bats* all!

LETTERS TO THE EDITOR

Dear Editor:
We know there are almost 1,000 different kinds of bats living in the world today. There are more types of bats than almost any other kind of mammal. Most of them eat pollen, nectar, fruit, frogs, fish, other bats, and even lizards!
So how come you only had one kind of bat in your book?

Signed,
BLA (Bat Lovers of America)

Dear Bat Lovers of America,
We didn't have enough pages to include all those bats in one book! Besides, we couldn't do a story about lizard-eating bats. Imagine how Liz would feel!
—The Editor

Dear Editor,
Listen up! I know for a fact that humans can't really hear the sounds bats use to echolate—they are too high-pitched for us to hear!

Best wishes,
An Ear-ly Rising Fan

We hear ya! And you are absolutely right.
—The Editor

Dear Editor,
For your information, there are three kinds of bats that feed on blood. They make a tiny cut in an animal and lap up whatever blood drips out. They are called vampire bats. But they got that name from people who loved make-believe vampire stories.

Sincerely,
The Transylvanian Trio

Fangs for the information!
—The Editor

A Note to Parents, Teachers, and Kids

Poor bats. They are such misunderstood creatures. Read on to find out more...

1. Are bats birds?

Surprise! Bats are mammals just like us. That means their bodies are covered with fur, their young are born live, and they nurse their young on milk produced by the mother.

2. Are bats blind?

Lots of people use the expression "blind as a bat." But just because bats shy away from direct light doesn't mean they are blind. The truth is, the majority of bats can see as well as humans.

3. Do bats give people rabies?

People tend to stay away from bats because they fear they can get rabies from them. The truth is, most bats do not have rabies, but some (particularly the silver-winged bat) do. And since you can't tell whether or not a bat is healthy, the best thing to do is to keep your distance from them, the way you should from any wild animal. And if you see an injured bat lying still, don't go near it. Instead, call the animal control center nearest you. The animal will probably die, and the experts will know how to dispose of it.

4. Are bats cruel animals?

Actually, bats are very social, loving creatures. Mother bats spend most of their time tending to their young. And should a baby bat become abandoned, a mother bat will adopt the orphaned bat and care for it as her own.

Ms. Frizzle